The Lottery

MARIA EDGEWORTH

A Phoenix Paperback

This edition published in 1996 by Phoenix
a division of Orion Books Ltd
Orion House, 5 Upper St Martin's Lane, London WC2H 9EA

ISBN 1 85799 759 X

Typeset by Deltatype Ltd, Ellesmere Port, Cheshire
Printed in Great Britain by Clays Ltd, St Ives plc

The Lottery

CHAPTER 1

Near Derby, on the way towards Darley-grove, there is a cottage which formerly belonged to one Maurice Robinson. The jessamine which now covers the porch was planted by Ellen, his wife: she was an industrious, prudent, young woman; liked by all her neighbours, because she was ready to assist and serve them, and the delight of her husband's heart; for she was sweet-tempered, affectionate, constantly clean and neat, and made his house so cheerful that he was always in haste to come home to her, after his day's work. He was one of the manufacturers employed in the cotton works at Derby; and he was remarkable for his good conduct and regular attendance at his work.

Things went on very well in every respect, till a relation of his, Mrs Dolly Robinson, came to live with him. Mrs Dolly had been laundry-maid in a great family, where she learned to love gossiping, and tea-drinkings, and where she acquired some taste for shawls and cherry-brandy. She thought that she did her young relations a great favour by coming to take up her abode with them, because, as she observed, they were young and inexperienced; and she, knowing a great deal of the world, was able and willing to advise them; and besides, she had had a legacy of some hundred pounds left to her, and she had saved some little matters while in service, which might make it worth her relations' while to take her advice with proper respect, and to make her comfortable for the rest of her days.

Ellen treated her with all due deference, and endeavoured to make her as comfortable as possible; but Mrs Dolly could not be comfortable unless, besides drinking a large spoonful of brandy in every dish of tea, she could make each person in the house do just what she pleased. She began by being dissatisfied because she could not persuade Ellen that brandy was wholesome, in tea, for the nerves; next she was affronted because Ellen did not admire her shawl; and, above all, she was grievously offended because Ellen endeavoured to prevent her from spoiling little George.

George was, at this time, between five and six years old; and his mother took a great deal of pains to bring him up well: she endeavoured to teach him to be honest, to speak the truth, to do whatever she and his father bid him, and to dislike being idle.

Mrs Dolly, on the contrary, coaxed and flattered him, without caring whether he was obedient or disobedient, honest or dishonest. She was continually telling him that he was the finest little fellow in the world; and that she would do great things for him, some time or another.

What these great things were to be the boy seemed neither to know nor care; and, except at the moments when she was stuffing gingerbread into his mouth, he seemed never to desire to be near her: he preferred being with William Deane, his father's friend, who was a very ingenious man, and whom he liked to see at work.

William gave him a slate, and a slate pencil; and taught him how to make figures, and to cast up sums; and made a little wheel-barrow for him, of which George was very fond, so that George called him in play 'King Deane.' All these things tended to make Mrs Dolly dislike William Deane, whom she considered as her rival in power.

One day, it was George's birthday, Mrs Dolly invited a party, as she called it, to drink tea with her; and, at tea-time, she was entertaining the neighbours with stories of what she had seen in the great world. Amongst others, 3 she had a favourite story of a butler, in the family where she had lived, who bought a ticket in the lottery when he was drunk, which ticket came up a ten thousand pound prize when he was sober; and the butler turned gentleman, and kept his coach directly.

One evening, Maurice Robinson and William came home, after their day's work, just in time to hear the end of this story; and Mrs Dolly concluded it by turning to Maurice, and assuring him that he must put into the lottery and try his luck: for why should not he be as lucky as another? 'Here,' said she, 'a man is working and drudging all the days of his life to get a decent coat to put on, and a bit of bread to put into his child's mouth; and, after all, may be he can't do it; though all the while, for five guineas, or a guinea, or half-a-guinea even, if he has but the spirit to lay out his money properly, he has the chance of making a fortune without any trouble. Surely a man should try his luck, if not for his own, at least for his children's sake,' continued Mrs Dolly, drawing little George towards her, and hugging him in her arms. 'Who knows what might turn up! Make your papa buy a ticket in the lottery, love; there's my darling; and I'll be bound he'll have good luck. Tell him, I'll be bound we shall have a ten thousand pound prize at least; and all for a few guineas. I'm sure I think none but a miser would grudge the money, if he had it to give.'

As Mrs Dolly finished her speech, she looked at William Deane, whose countenance did not seem to please her. Maurice was whistling, and Ellen knitting as fast as possible. Little George was counting William Deane's buttons. 'Pray, Mr Deane,' cried Mrs Dolly, turning full upon him, 'what may your advice and opinion be? since nothing's to be done here without your leave and word of command, forsooth. Now, as you know so much and have seen so much of the world, would you be pleased to tell this good company, and myself into the bargain, what harm it can do anybody, but a miser, to lay out a small sum to get a good chance of a round thousand, or five thousand, or ten thousand, or twenty thousand pounds, without more ado?'

As she pronounced the words five thousand, ten thousand, twenty thousand pounds, in a triumphant voice, all the company, except Ellen and William, seemed to feel the force of her oratory.

William coolly answered that he was no miser, but that he thought money might be better laid out than in the lottery; for that there was more chance of a man's getting nothing for his money than of his getting a prize; that when a man worked for fair wages every day, he was sure of getting something for his pains, and with honest industry, and saving, might get rich enough in time, and have to thank himself for it, which would be a pleasant thing: but that if a man, as he had known many, set his heart upon the turning of the lottery wheel, he would leave off putting his hand to any thing the whole year round, and so grow idle, and may be, drunken; 'and then,' said William, 'at the year's end, if he have a blank, what is he to do for his rent, or for his wife and children, that have nothing to depend upon but him and his industry?'

Here Maurice sighed, and so did Ellen, whilst William went on and told many a true story of honest servants, and tradesmen, whom he had known, who had ruined themselves by gaming and lotteries.

'But,' said Maurice, who now broke silence, 'putting into the lottery, William, is not gaming, like dice or cards, or such things. Putting into the lottery is not gaming, as I take it.'

'As I take it, though,' replied William, 'it is gaming. For what is gaming but trusting one's money, or somewhat, to luck and hap-hazard? And is there not as much hap-hazard in the turning of the wheel as in the coming up of the dice, or the dealing of the cards?'

'True enough; but somebody must get a prize,' argued

Maurice.

'And somebody must win at dice or cards,' said William, 'but a many more must lose; and a many more, I take it, must lose by the lottery than by any other game; else how would they that keep the lottery gain by it, as they do? Put a case. If you and I, Maurice, were this minute to play at dice, we stake our money down on the table here, and one or t'other takes all up. But, in the lottery, it is another affair; for the whole of what is put in does never come out.'

This statement of the case made some impression upon Maurice, who was no fool; but Mrs Dolly's desire that he should buy a lottery ticket, was not to be conquered by reason: it grew stronger and stronger the more she was opposed. She was silent and cross during the remainder of the evening; and the next morning, at breakfast, she was so low that even her accustomed dose of brandy, in her tea, had no effect.

Now Maurice, besides his confused hopes that Mrs Dolly would leave something handsome to him or his family, thought himself obliged to her for having given a helping hand to his father, when he was in distress; and therefore he wished to bear with her humours, and to make her happy in his house. He knew that the lottery ticket was uppermost in her mind, and the moment he touched upon that subject she brightened up. She told 7 him she had had a dream; and she had great faith in dreams: and she had dreamed, three times over, that he had bought number 339 in the lottery, and that it had come up a ten thousand pound prize!

'Well, Ellen,' said Maurice, 'I've half a mind to try my luck; and it can do us no harm, for I'll only put off buying the cow this year.'

'Nay,' said Mrs Dolly, 'why so? may be you don't know what I know, that Ellen's as rich as a Jew? She has a cunning little cupboard, in the wall yonder, that I see her putting money into every day of her life, and none goes out.'

Ellen immediately went and drew back a small sliding oak door in the wainscot, and took out a glove, in which some money was wrapped; she put it altogether in her husband's hand, saying with a good-humoured smile, 'There is my year's spinning, Maurice: I only thought to have made more of it before I gave it you. Do what you please with it.'

Maurice was so much moved by his wife's kindness, that he at the moment determined to give up his lottery scheme, of which, he knew, she did not approve. But, though a good-natured, well-meaning man, he was of an irresolute character; and even when he saw what was best to be done, had not courage to persist. As he was coming home from work, a few days after Ellen had given him the money, he saw, in one of the streets of Derby, a house with large windows finely illuminated, and read the words 'Lottery-office of Fortunatus, Gould, and Co. At this office was sold the fortunate ticket, which came up on Monday last a twenty thousand pound prize. Ready money paid for prizes immediately on demand,

The 15,000*l*.

10,000*l*.

5,000*l*.

still in the wheel. None but the brave deserve a prize.'

Whilst Maurice was gazing at this and other similar advertisements, which were exhibited in various bright colours in this tempting window, his desire to try his fortune in the lottery returned; and he was just going into the office to purchase a ticket, when luckily he found that he had not his leathern purse in his pocket. He walked on, and presently brushed by some one; it was William Deane, who was looking very eagerly over some old books, at a bookseller's stall. 'I wish I had but money to treat myself with some of these,' said William: 'but I cannot; they cost such a deal of money, having all these prints in them.'

'We can lend you, – no, we can't neither,' cried

Maurice, stopping himself short; for he recollected that he could not both lend his friend money to buy the books and buy a lottery ticket. He was in great doubt which he should do; and walked on with William, in silence. 'So, then,' cried he at last, 'you would not advise me to put into the lottery?'

'Nay,' said William laughing, 'it is not for me to advise you about it, now; for I know you are considering whether you had best put it into the lottery or lend me the money to buy these books. Now, I hope you don't think I was looking to my own interest in what I said the other day; for I can assure you, I had no thoughts of meeting with these books at that time, and did not know that you had any money to spare.'

'Say no more about it,' replied Maurice. 'Don't I know you are an honest fellow, and would lend me the money if I wanted it? You shall have it as soon as ever we get home. Only mind and stand by me stoutly, if Mrs Dolly begins any more about the lottery.'

Mrs Dolly did not fail to renew her attacks; and she was both provoked and astonished when she found that the contents of the leathern purse were put into the hands of William Deane.

'Books, indeed! To buy books forsooth! What business had such a one as he with books?' She had seen a deal of life, she said, and never saw no good come of bookish bodies; and she was sorry to see that her own darling, George, was taking to the bookish line, and that his mother encouraged him in it. She would lay her best shawl, she said, to a gauze handkerchief, that William Deane would, sooner or later, beggar himself, and all that belonged to him, by his books and his gimcracks; 'and if George were my son,' continued she, raising her voice, 'I'd soon cure him of prying and poring into that man's picture-books, and following him up and down with wheels and mechanic machines, which will never come to no good, nor never make a gentleman of him, as a ticket in the lottery might and would.'

All mouths were open at once to defend William. Maurice declared he was the most industrious man in the parish; that his books never kept him from his work, but always kept him from the alehouse and bad company; and that, as to his gimcracks and machines, he never laid out a farthing upon them but what he got by working on holidays, and odd times, when other folks were idling or tippling. His master, who understood the like of those things, said, before all the workmen at the mills, that William Deane's machines were main clever, and might come to bring in a deal of money for him and his.

'Why,' continued Maurice, 'there was Mr Arkwright, the man that first set a going all our cotton frames here, was no better than William Deane, and yet came at last to make a power of money. It stands to reason, any how, that William Deane is hurting nobody, nor himself neither; and, moreover, he may divert himself his own way, without being taken to task by man, woman, or child. As to children, he's very good to my child; there's one loves him,' pointing to George, 'and I'm glad of it: for I should be ashamed, so I should, that my flesh and blood should be in any ways disregardful or ungracious to those that be kind and good to them.'

Mrs Dolly, swelling with anger, repeated in a scornful voice, 'Disregardful, ungracious! I wonder folks can talk so to me! but this is all the gratitude one meets with, in this world, for all one does. Well, well! I'm an old woman, and shall soon be out of people's way; and then they will be sorry they did not use me better; and then they'll bethink them that it is not so easy to gain a friend as to lose a friend; and then – '

Here Mrs Dolly's voice was stopped by her sobs; and Maurice, who was a very good-natured man, and much disposed to gratitude, said he begged her pardon a thousand times, if he had done any thing to offend her; and declared his only wish was to please and satisfy her, if she would but tell him how.

She continued sobbing, without making any answer, for some time: but at last she cried, 'My ad- my ad- my ad-vice is never taken in any thing!'

Maurice declared he was ready to take her advice, if that was the only way to make her easy in her mind. 'I know what you mean, now,' added he: 'you are still harping upon the lottery ticket. Well, I'll buy a ticket this day week, after I've sold the cow I bought at the fair. Will you have done sobbing, now, cousin Dolly?'

'Indeed, cousin Maurice, it is only for your own sake I speak,' said she, wiping her eyes. 'You know you was always a favourite of mine from your childhood up; I nursed you, and had you on my knee, and foretold often and often you would make a fortune, so I did. And will you buy the ticket I dreamed about, hey?'

Maurice assured her that, if it was to be had, he would. The cow was accordingly sold the following week, and the ticket in the lottery was bought. It was not, however, the number about which Mrs Dolly had dreamed, for that was already purchased by some other person. The ticket Maurice bought was number 80; and, after he had got it, his cousin Dolly continually deplored that it was not the very number of which she dreamed. It would have been better not to have taken her advice at all than to have taken it when it was too late.

Maurice was an easy-tempered man, and loved quiet; and when he found that he was reproached for something or other whenever he came into his own house, he began to dislike the thought of going home after his day's work, and loitered at public-houses sometimes, but more frequently at the lottery-office. As the lottery was now drawing, his whole thoughts were fixed upon his ticket; and he neglected his work at the manufactory. 'What signify a few shillings wages, more or less?' said he to himself. 'If my ticket should come up a prize, it makes a rich man of me at once.'

His ticket at last was drawn a prize of five thousand pounds! He was almost out of his senses with joy! He ran home to tell the news. 'A prize! a prize, Dolly!' cried he, as soon as he had breath to speak.

'That comes of taking my advice!' said Dolly.

'A five thousand pound prize! my dear Ellen,' cried he, and down he kicked her spinning-wheel.

'I wish we may be as happy with it as we have been without it, Maurice,' said Ellen; and calmly lifted her spinning-wheel up again.

'No more spinning-wheels!' cried Maurice; 'no more spinning! no more work! We have nothing to do now but to be as happy as the day is long. Wife, I say, put by that wheel.'

'You're a lady now; and ought to look and behave like a lady,' added Mrs Dolly, stretching up her head, 'and not stand moping over an old spinning-wheel.'

'I don't know how to look and behave like a lady,' said Ellen, and sighed: 'but I hopes Maurice won't love me the less for that.'

Mrs Dolly was for some time wholly taken up with the pleasure of laying out money, and 'preparing,' as she said, 'to look like somebody.' She had many acquaintances at Paddington, she said, and she knew of a very snug house there, where they could all live very *genteel*.

She was impatient to go thither for two reasons; that she might make a figure in the eyes of these acquaintances, and that she might get Maurice and little George away from William Deane, who was now become more than ever the object of her aversion and contempt; for he actually advised his friend not to think of living in idleness, though he had five thousand pounds. William moreover recommended it to him to put his money out to interest, or to dispose of a good part of it in stocking a farm, or in fitting out a shop. Ellen, being a farmer's daughter, knew well the management of a dairy; and, when a girl, had also assisted in a haberdasher's shop, that was kept in Derby by her uncle; so she was able and willing, she said, to assist her husband in whichever of these ways of life he should take to.

Maurice, irresolute and desirous of pleasing all parties, at last said, it would be as well, seeing they were now rich enough not to mind such a journey, just to go to Paddington and look about 'em; and if so be they could not settle there in comfort, why still they might see a bit of London town, and take their pleasure for a month or so; and he hoped William Deane would come along with them, and it should not be a farthing out of his pocket.

Little George said every thing he could think of to persuade his *King Deane* to go with them, and almost pulled him to the coach door, when they were setting off; but William could not leave his master and his business. The child clung with his legs and arms so fast to him that they were forced to drag him into the carriage.

'You'll find plenty of friends at Paddington, who'll give you many pretty things. Dry your eyes, and see! you're in a coach!' said Mrs Dolly.

George dried his eyes directly, for he was ashamed of crying; but he answered, 'I don't care for your pretty things. I shall not find my good dear King Deane any where;' and, leaning upon his mother's lap, he twirled round the wheel of a little cart, which William Deane had given him, and which he carried under his arm as his greatest treasure.

Ellen was delighted to see signs of such a grateful and affectionate disposition in her son, and all her thoughts were bent upon him; whilst Mrs Dolly chattered on about her acquaintance at Paddington, and her satisfaction at finding herself in a coach once again. Her satisfaction was not, however, of long continuance; for she grew so sick that she was obliged, or thought herself obliged, every quarter of an hour, to have recourse to her cordial bottle. Her spirits were at last raised so much, that she became extremely communicative, and she laid open to Maurice and Ellen all her plans of future pleasure and expense.

'In the first place,' said she, 'I am heartily glad now I have got you away from that cottage that was not fit to live in; and from certain folks that shall be nameless, that would have one live all one's life like scrubs, like themselves. You must know that when we get to Paddington, the first thing I shall do shall be to buy a handsome coach.'

'A coach!' exclaimed Maurice and Ellen, with extreme astonishment.

'A coach, to be sure,' said Mrs Dolly. 'I say a coach.'

'I say we shall be ruined, then,' said Maurice; 'and laughed at into the bargain.'

'La! you don't know what money is,' said Mrs Dolly. 'Why haven't you five thousand pounds, man! You don't know what can be done with five thousand pounds, cousin Maurice.'

'No, nor you neither, cousin Dolly; or you'd never talk of setting up your coach.'

'Why not, pray? I know what a coach costs as well as another. I know we can have a second-hand coach, and we need not tell nobody that it's second-hand, for about a hundred pounds. And what's a hundred pounds out of five thousand?'

'But if we've a coach, we must have horses, must not we?' said Ellen, 'and they'll cost a hundred more.'

'Oh, we can have job horses, that will cost us little or nothing,' said Mrs Dolly.

'Say 150*l.* a-year,' replied Maurice; 'for I heard my master's coachman telling that the livery-keeper in London declared as how he made nothing by letting him have job horses for 150*l.* a-year.'

'We are to have our own coach,' said Dolly, 'and that will be cheaper, you know.'

'But the coach won't last for ever,' said Ellen; 'it must 18 be mended, and that will cost something.'

'It is time enough to think of that when the coach wants mending,' said Mrs Dolly; who, without giving herself the trouble of calculating, seemed to be convinced that every thing might be done for five thousand pounds. 'I must let you know a little secret,' continued she. 'I have written, that is, got a friend to write, to have the house at Paddington taken for a year; for I know it's quite the thing for us, and we are only to give fifty pounds a-year for it: and you know that one thousand pounds would pay that rent for twenty years to come.'

'But then,' said Ellen, 'you will want to do a great many other things with that thousand pounds. There's the coach you mentioned; and you said we must keep a footboy, and must see a deal of company, and must not grudge to buy clothes and that we could not follow any trade, nor have a farm, nor do any thing to make money; so we must live on upon what we have. Now let us count, and see how we shall do it. You know, Maurice, that William Deane inquired about what we could get for our five thousand pounds, if we put it out to interest?'

'Ay; two hundred a-year, he said.'

'Well, we pay fifty pounds a-year for the rent of the house, and a hundred a-year we three and the boy must have to live upon, and there is but fifty pounds a-year left.'

Mrs Dolly, with some reluctance, gave up the notion of the coach; and Ellen proposed that five hundred pounds should be laid out in furnishing a haberdasher's shop, and that the rest of their money should be put out to interest, till it was wanted. 'Maurice and I can take care of the shop very well; and we can live well enough upon what we make by it,' said Ellen.

Mrs Dolly opposed the idea of keeping a shop; and observed that they should not, in that case, be gentle-folks. Besides, she said, she was sure the people of the house she had taken would never let it be turned into a shop.

What Mrs Dolly had said was indeed true. When they got to Paddington, they found that the house was by no means fit for a shop; and as the bargain was made for a year, and they could not get it off their hands without considerable loss, Ellen was forced to put off her prudent scheme. In the mean time she determined to learn how to keep accounts properly.

There was a small garden belonging to the house, in which George set to work; and though he could do little more than pull up the weeds, yet this kept him out of mischief and idleness; and she sent him to a day-school, where he would learn to read, write, and cast accounts.

When he came home in the evenings, he used to show her his copy-book, and read his lesson, and say his spelling to her, while she was at work. His master said it was a pleasure to teach him, he was so eager to learn; and Ellen was glad that she had money enough to pay for having her boy well taught. Mrs Dolly, all this time, was sitting and gossiping amongst her acquaintance in Paddington. These acquaintance were people whom she had seen when they visited the housekeeper in the great family where she was laundry-maid; and she was very proud to show them that she was now a finer person then even the housekeeper, who was formerly the object of her envy. She had tea-drinking parties, and sometimes dinner parties, two or three in a week; and hired a footboy, and laughed at Ellen for her low notions, and dissuaded Maurice from all industrious schemes; still saying to him, 'Oh, you'll have time enough to think of going to work when you have spent all your money.'

Maurice, who had been accustomed to be at work for several hours in the day, at first thought it would be a fine thing to walk about, as Mrs Dolly said, like a gentleman, without having any thing to do; but when he came to try it, he found himself more tired by this way of life than he had ever felt himself in the cotton-mills at Derby. He gaped and gaped, and lounged about every morning, and looked a hundred times at his new watch, and put it to his ear to listen whether it was going, the time seemed to him to pass so slowly. Sometimes he sauntered through the town, came back again, and stood at his own door looking at dogs fighting for a bone; at others, he went into the kitchen, to learn what there was to be for dinner, and to watch the maid cooking, or the boy cleaning knives. It was a great relief for him to go into the room where his wife was at work: but he never would have been able to get through a year in this way without the assistance of a pretty little black horse, for which he paid thirty guineas. During a month he was very happy in riding backwards and forwards on the Edgeware-road: but presently the horse fell lame; it was discovered that he was spavined and broken-winded; and the jockey from whom Maurice bought him was no where to be found. Maurice sold the horse for five guineas, and bought a fine bay for forty, which he was certain would turn out well, seeing he paid such a good price for him; but the bay scarcely proved better than the black. How he managed it we do not know, but it seems he was not so skilful in horses as in cotton-weaving; for at the end of the year he had no horse, and had lost fifty guineas by his bargains.

Another hundred guineas were gone, nobody in the

family but himself knew how: but he resolved to waste no more money and began the new year well, by opening a haberdasher's shop in Paddington. The fitting up this shop cost them five hundred pounds; it was tolerably stocked, and Ellen was so active, and so attentive to all customers, that she brought numbers to Maurice Robinson's new shop. They made full twelve per cent upon all they sold; and in six months, had turned three hundred pounds twice, and had gained the profit of seventy-two pounds. Maurice, however, had got such a habit of lounging, during his year of idleness, that he could not relish steady attendance in the shop: he was often out, frequently came home late at night, and Ellen observed that he sometimes looked extremely melancholy; but when she asked him whether he was ill, or what ailed him, he always turned away, answering, 'Nothing – nothing ails me. Why do ye fancy any thing ails me?'

Alas! it was no fancy. Ellen saw too plainly, that something was going wrong: but as her husband persisted in silence, she could not tell how to assist or comfort him.

Mrs Dolly in the mean time was going on spending her money in junketing. She was, besides, no longer satisfied with taking her spoonful of brandy in every dish of tea; she found herself uncomfortable, she said, unless she took every morning fasting a full glass of good cordial recommended to her by her friend, Mrs Joddrell, the apothecary's wife. Now this good cordial, in plain English, was a strong dram. Ellen, in the gentlest manner she could, represented to Mrs Dolly that she was hurting her health, and was exposing herself, by this increasing habit of drinking; but she replied with anger, that what she *took* was for the good of her health; that everybody knew best what agreed with them; that she should trust to her own feelings; and that nobody need talk, when all she took came out of the apothecary's shop, and was paid for honestly with her own money.

Besides what came out of the apothecary's shop, Mrs Dolly found it agreed with her constantly to drink a pot of porter at dinner, and another at supper; and always when she had a cold, and she had often a cold, she drank large basins full of white wine whey, 'to throw off her cold,' as she said.

Then by degrees, she lost her appetite, and found she could eat nothing, unless she had a glass of brandy at dinner. Small beer, she discovered, did not agree with her; so at luncheon time she always had a tumbler full of brandy and water. This she carefully mixed herself, and put less water in evey day, because brandy, she was

convinced, was more wholesome for some constitutions

than water; and brandy and peppermint, taken together, was an infallible remedy for all complaints, low spirits included.

CHAPTER II

Mrs Dolly never found herself comfortable, moreover, unless she dined abroad two or three days in the week, at a public-house, near Paddington, where she said she was more at home than she was any where else. There was a bowling-green at this public-house, and it was a place to which tea-drinking parties resorted. Now Mrs Dolly often wanted to take little George out with her to these parties, and said, 'It is a pity and shame to keep the poor thing always mewed up at home, without ever letting him have any pleasure! Would not you like to go with me, George dear, in the one-horse chaise? and would not you be glad to have cakes, and tea, and all the good things that are to be had?'

'I should like to go in the one-horse chaise, to be sure, and to have cakes and tea; but I should not like to go with you, because mother does not choose it,' answered George, in his usual plain way of speaking. Ellen, who had often seen Mrs Dolly offer him wine and punch to drink, by way of a treat, was afraid he might gradually learn to love spirituous liquors; and that if he acquired a habit of drinking such when he was a boy, he would become a drunkard when he should grow to be a man. George was now almost nine years old; and he could understand the reason why his mother desired that he would not drink spirituous liquors. She once pointed out to him a drunken man, who was reeling along the street, and bawling ridiculous nonsense: he had quite lost his senses, and as he did not attend to the noise of a carriage coming fast behind him, he could not get out of the way time enough, and the coachman could not stop his horses; so the drunken man was thrown down, and the wheel of the carriage went over his leg, and broke it in a shocking manner. George saw him carried towards his home, writhing and groaning with pain. 'See what comes of drunkenness!' said Ellen.

She stopped the people, who were carrying the hurt man past her door, and had him brought in and laid upon a bed, whilst a surgeon was sent for. George stood beside the bed in silence; and the words 'See what comes of drunkenness!' sounded in his ears.

Another time, his mother pointed out to him a man

with terribly swollen legs, and a red face blotched all

over, lifted out of a fine coach by two footmen in fine liveries. The man leaned upon a gold-headed cane, after he was lifted from his carriage, and tried with his other hand to take off his hat to a lady, who asked him how he did; but his hand shook so much that, when he had got his hat off, he could not put it rightly upon his head, and his footman put it on for him. The boys in the street laughed at him. 'Poor man!' said Ellen; 'that is Squire L——, who, as you heard the apothecary say, has drunk harder in his day than any man that ever he knew; and this is what he has brought himself to by drinking! All the physic in the apothecary's shop cannot make him well again! No; nor can his fine coach and fine footmen any more make him easy or happy, poor man!'

George exclaimed, 'I wonder how people can be such fools as to be drunkards! I will never be a drunkard, mother; and now I know the reason why you desired me not to drink the wine, when Mrs Dolly used to say to me, "Down with it, George dear, it will do ye no harm." '

These circumstances made such an impression upon George that there was no further occasion to watch him; he always pushed away the glass when Mrs Dolly filled it for him.

One day his mother said to him, 'Now I can trust you to take care of yourself, George, I shall not watch you. 27

Mrs Dolly is going to a bowling-green tea-party this evening, and has asked you to go with her; and I have told her you shall.'

George accordingly went with Mrs Dolly to the bowling-green. The company drank tea out of doors, in summer-houses. After tea, Mrs Dolly bid George go and look at the bowling-green; and George was very well entertained with seeing the people playing at bowls; but when it grew late in the evening, and when the company began to go away, George looked about for Mrs Dolly. She was not in the summer-house, where they had drunk tea, nor was she any where upon the terrace round the bowling-green; so he went to the public-house in search of her, and at last found her standing at the bar with the landlady. Her face was very red, and she had a large glass of brandy in her hand, into which the landlady was pouring some drops, which she said were excellent for the stomach.

Mrs Dolly started so when she saw George, that she threw down half her glass of brandy. 'Bless us, child! I thought you were safe at the bowling-green,' said she.

'I saw every body going away,' answered George; 'so I thought it was time to look for you, and to go home.'

'But before you go, my dear little gentleman,' said the landlady, 'you must eat one of these tarts, for my sake.'

As she spoke, she gave George a little tart: 'and here,' added she, 'you must drink my health too in something good. Don't be afraid, love; it's nothing that will hurt you: it's very sweet and nice.'

'It is wine, or spirits of some sort or other, I know by the smell,' said George; 'and I will not drink it, thank you, ma'am.'

'The boy's a fool!' said Mrs Dolly; 'but it's his mother's fault. She won't let him taste any thing stronger than water. But now your mother's not by, you know,' said Mrs Dolly, winking at the landlady; 'now your mother's not by – '

'Yes, and nobody will tell of you,' added the landlady; 'so do what you like: drink it down, love.'

'No!' cried George, pushing away the glass which Mrs Dolly held to his lips. 'No! no! no! I say. I will not do any thing now my mother's not by, that I would not do if she was here in this room.'

'Well; hush, hush; and don't bawl so loud though,' said Mrs Dolly, who saw, what George did not see, a gentleman that was standing at the door of the parlour opposite to them, and who could hear every thing that was saying at the bar.

'I say,' continued George, in a loud voice, 'mother told me she could trust me to take care of myself; and so I 29 will take care of myself; and I am not a fool, no more is mother, I know; for she told me the reasons why it is not good to drink spirituous – .' Mrs Dolly pushed him away, without giving him time to finish his sentence, bidding him go and see whether the gig was ready; for it was time to be going home.

As George was standing in the yard, looking at the mechanism of the one-horse chaise and observing how the horse was put to, somebody tapped him upon the shoulder, and looking up, he saw a gentleman with a very good-natured countenance, who smiled upon him, and asked him whether he was the little boy who had just been talking so loud in the bar?

'Yes, sir,' says George. 'You seem to be a good little boy,' added he; 'and I liked what I heard you say very much. So you will not do any thing when your mother is not by, that you would not do if she was here – was not that what you said?'

'Yes, sir; as well as I remember.'

'And who is your mother?' continued the gentleman. 'Where does she live?'

George told him his mother's name, and where she lived; and the gentleman said, 'I will call at your mother's house as I go home, and tell her what I heard you say; and I will ask her to let you come to my house, where you will see a little boy of your own age, whom I should be very glad to have seen behave as well as you did just now.'

Mr Belton, for that was the name of the gentleman who took notice of George, was a rich carpet manufacturer. He had a country-house near Paddington; and the acquaintance which was thus begun became a source of great happiness to George. Mr Belton lent him several entertaining books, and took him to see many curious things in London. Ellen was rejoiced to hear from him the praises of her son. All the pleasure of Ellen's life had, for some months past, depended upon this boy; for her husband was seldom at home, and the gloom that was spread over his countenance alarmed her, whenever she saw him. As for Mrs Dolly, she was no companion for Ellen: her love of drinking had increased to such a degree that she could love nothing else; and when she was not half intoxicated, she was in such low spirits that she sat (either on the side of her bed, or in her arm-chair, wrapped in a shawl) sighing and crying, and see-sawing herself; and sometimes she complained to Maurice that Ellen did not care whether she was dead or alive; and at others that George had always something or other to do, and never liked to sit in her room and keep her company. Besides all this, she got into a hundred petty quarrels with the neighbours, who had a knack of remembering what she said when she was drunk, and appealing to her for satisfaction when she was sober. Mrs Dolly regularly expected that Ellen should, as she called it, stand her friend in these altercations; to which Ellen could not always in justice consent. Ah! said Ellen to herself one night, as she was sitting up late waiting for her husband's return home, it is not the having five thousand pounds that makes people happy! When Maurice loved to come home after his day's work to our little cottage, and when our George was his delight, as he is mine, then I was light of heart; but now it is quite otherwise. However, there is no use in complaining, nor in sitting down to think upon melancholy things; and Ellen started up and went to work, to mend one of her husband's waistcoats.

Whilst she was at this employment, she listened continually for the return of Maurice. The clock struck twelve, and one, and no husband came! She heard no noise in the street when she opened her window, for every body but herself was in bed and asleep. At last she heard the sound of footsteps; but it was so dark that she could not see who the person was, who continued walking backwards and forwards, just underneath the window.

'Is it you, Maurice? Are you there, Maurice?' said Ellen. The noise of the footsteps ceased, and Ellen again said, 'Is it you, Maurice? Are you there?'

'Yes,' answered Maurice: 'it is I. Why are you not abed and asleep, at this time of night?'

'I am waiting for you,' replied Ellen.

'You need not wait for me; I have the key of the house door in my pocket, and can let myself in whenever I choose it.'

'And don't you choose it now?' said Ellen.

'No. Shut down the window.'

Ellen shut the window, and went and sat down upon the side of her boy's bed. He was sleeping. Ellen, who could not sleep, took up her work again, and resolved to wait till her husband should come in. At last, the key turned in the house door, and presently she heard her husband's steps coming softly towards the room where she was sitting. He opened the door gently, as if he expected to find her asleep, and was afraid of awakening her. He started when he saw her; and slouching his hat over his face, threw himself into a chair without speaking a single word. Something terrible has happened to him, surely! thought Ellen; and her hand trembled so that she could scarcely hold her needle, when she tried to go on working.

'What are you doing there, Ellen?' said he, suddenly pushing back his hat.

'I'm only mending your waistcoat, love,' said Ellen, in a faltering voice.

'I am a wretch! a fool! a miserable wretch!' exclaimed Maurice, starting up and striking his forehead with violence as he walked up and down the room.

'What can be the matter?' said Ellen. 'It is worse to me to see you in this way, than to hear whatever misfortune has befallen you. Don't turn away from me, husband! Who in the world loves you so well as I do?'

'Oh, Ellen,' said he, letting her take his hand, but still turning away, 'you will hate me when you know what I have done.'

'I cannot hate you, I believe,' said Ellen.

'We have not sixpence left in the world!' continued Maurice, vehemently. 'We must leave this house to-morrow; we must sell all we have; I must go to jail, Ellen! You must work all the rest of your days harder than ever you did; and so must that poor boy, who lies sleeping yonder. He little thinks that his father has made a beggar of him; and that, whilst his mother was the best of mothers to him, his father was ruining him, her, and himself, with a pack of rascals at the gaming-table. Ellen, I have lost every shilling of our money!'

'Is that all?' said Ellen. 'That's bad; but I am glad that you have done nothing wicked. We can work hard, and be happy again. Only promise me now, dear husband, that you will never game any more.'

Maurice threw himself upon his knees, and swore that he never, to the last hour of his life, would go to any gaming-table again, or play at any game of chance. Ellen then said all she could to soothe and console him; she persuaded him to take some rest, of which he was much in need, for his looks were haggard, and he seemed quite exhausted. He declared that he had not had a night's sleep for many months, since he had got into these difficulties by gaming. His mind had been kept in a continual flurry, and he seemed as if he had been living in a fever. 'The worst of it was, Ellen,' said he, 'I could not bear to see you or the boy when I had been losing; so I went on, gaming deeper and deeper, in hopes of winning back what I had lost; and I now and then won, and they coaxed me and told me I was getting a run of luck, and it would be a sin to turn my back on good fortune. This way I was 'ticed to go on playing, till, when I betted higher and higher, my luck left me; or, as I shrewdly suspect, the rascals did not play fair, and they won stake after stake, till they made me half mad, and I risked all I had left upon one throw, and lost it! And 35 when I found I had lost all, and thought of coming home to you and our boy, I was ready to hang myself. Oh, Ellen, if you knew all I have felt! I would not live over again the last two years for this room full of gold!'

Such are the miserable feelings, and such the life, of a gamester!

Maurice slept for a few hours, or rather dozed, starting now and then, and talking of cards and dice, and sometimes grinding his teeth and clenching his hand, till he wakened himself by the violence with which he struck the side of the bed.

'I have had a terrible dream, wife,' said he, when he opened his eyes, and saw Ellen sitting beside him on the bed. At first he did not recollect what had really happened; but as Ellen looked at him with sorrow and compassion in her countenance, he gradually remembered all the truth; and, hiding his head under the bedclothes, he said he wished he could sleep again, if it could be without dreaming such dreadful things.

It was in vain that he tried to sleep; so he got up, resolving to try whether he could borrow twenty guineas from any of his friends, to pay the most pressing of his gaming companions. The first person he asked was Mrs Dolly: she fell into an hysteric fit when she heard of his losses; and it was not till after she had swallowed a double dram of brandy that she was able to speak, and to tell him that she was the worst person in the world he could have applied to; for that she was in the greatest distress herself, and all her dependance in this world was upon him.

Maurice stood in silent astonishment. 'Why, cousin,' said he, 'I thought, and always believed, that you had a power of money! You know, when you came to live with us, you told me so.'

'No matter what I told you,' said Mrs Dolly. 'Folks can't live upon air. Yesterday the landlady of the public-house at the bowling-green, whom I'm sure I looked upon as my friend, – but there's no knowing one's friends, – sent me in a bill as long as my arm; and the apothecary here has another against me worse again; and the man at the livery-stables, for one-horse *chays*, and jobs that I'm sure I forgot ever having, comes and charges me the Lord knows what! and then the grocer for tea and sugar, which I have been giving to folks from whom I have got no thanks. And then I have an account with the linen-draper of I don't know how much! but he has over-charged me, I know, scandalously, for my last three shawls. And then I have never paid for my set of tea china; and half of the cups are broke, and the silver spoons, and I can't tell what besides.'

In short, Mrs Dolly, who had never kept any account of what she spent, had no idea how far she was getting into a tradesman's debt till his bill was brought home: and was in great astonishment to find, when all her bills were sent in, that she had spent four hundred and fifty pounds in her private expenses, drinking included, in the course of three years and eight months. She had now nothing left to live upon but one hundred pounds, so that she was more likely to be a burden to Maurice than any assistance. He, however, was determined to go to a friend, who had frequently offered to lend him any sum of money he might want, and who had often been his partner at the gaming-table.

In his absence, Ellen and George began to take a list of all the furniture in the house, that it might be ready for a sale, and Mrs Dolly sat in her arm-chair, weeping and wailing.

'Oh! laud! laud! that I should live to see all this!' cried she. 'Ah, lack-a-daisy! lack-a-daisy! lack-a-day! what will become of me! Oh, la! la! la!' Her lamentations were interrupted by a knock at the door. 'Hark! a knock, a double knock at the door,' cried Mrs Dolly. 'Who is it? Ah, lack-a-day, when people come to know what has happened, it will be long enough before we have any more visitors; long enough before we hear any more double knocks at the door. Oh, laud! laud! See who it is, George.'

It was Mr Belton, who was come to ask George to go with him and his little nephew to see some wild beasts at Exeter-'change: he was much surprised at the sorrowful faces of George and Ellen, whom he had always been used to see so cheerful, and inquired what misfortune had befallen them? Mrs Dolly thought she could tell the story best, so she detailed the whole, with many piteous ejaculations; but the silent resignation of Ellen's countenance had much more effect upon Mr Belton. 'George,' said he, 'must stay to finish the inventory he is writing for his mother.'

Mr Belton was inquiring more particularly into the amount of Maurice's debts, and the names of the persons to whom he had lost his money at the gaming-table, when the unfortunate man himself came home. 'No hope, Ellen!' cried he. 'No hope from any of those rascals that I thought my friends. No hope!'

He stopped short, seeing a stranger in the room, for Mr Belton was a stranger to him. 'My husband can tell you the names of all the people,' said Ellen, 'who have been the ruin of us.' Mr Belton then wrote them down from Maurice's information; and learned from him that he had lost to these sharpers upwards of three thousand eight hundred pounds in the course of three years; that the last night he played, he had staked the goods in his shop, valued at 350*l*., and lost them; that afterwards he staked the furniture of his house, valued at 160*l*.; this also he lost; and so left the gaming-table without a farthing in the world.

'It is not my intention,' said Mr Belton, 'to add to your present suffering, Mr Robinson, by pointing out that it has arisen entirely from your own imprudence. Nor yet can I say that I feel much compassion for you; for I have always considered a gamester as a most selfish being, who should be suffered to feel the terrible consequences of his own avaricious folly, as a warning to others.'

'Oh, sir! Oh, Mr Belton!' cried Ellen bursting now, for the first time, into tears, 'do not speak so harshly to Maurice.'

'To you I shall not speak harshly,' said Mr Belton, his voice and looks changing; 'for I have the greatest compassion for such an excellent wife and mother. And I shall take care that neither you nor your son, whom you have taken such successful pains to educate, shall suffer by the folly and imprudence in which you had no share. As to the ready money which your husband has lost and paid to these sharpers, it is, I fear, irrecoverable; but the goods in your shop, and the furniture in your house, I will take care shall not be touched. I will go immediately to my attorney, and direct him to inquire into the truth of all I have been told, and to prosecute these villains for keeping a gaming-table, and playing at unlawful games. Finish that inventory which you are making out, George, and give it to me; I will have the furniture in your house, Ellen, valued by an appraiser, and will advance you money to the amount, on which you may continue to live in comfort and credit, trusting to your industry and integrity to repay me in small sums, as you find it convenient, out of the profits of your shop.'

'Oh, sir!' cried Maurice, clasping his hands with a strong expression of joy, 'thank you! thank you from the bottom of my soul! Save her from misery, save the boy, and let me suffer as I ought for my folly.'

Mr Belton in spite of his contempt for gamesters, was touched by Maurice's repentance; but, keeping a steady countenance, replied in a firm tone, 'Suffering for folly does nobody any good, unless it makes them wiser in future.'

CHAPTER III

Mrs Dolly, who had been unaccountably awed to silence by Mr Belton's manner of speaking and looking, broke forth the moment he had left the house. 'Very genteel, indeed; though he might have taken more notice of me. See what it is, George, to have the luck of meeting with good friends.'

'See what it is to deserve good friends, George,' said Ellen.

'You'll all remember, I hope,' said Mrs Dolly, raising her voice, 'that it was I who was the first and foremost cause of all this, by taking George along with me to the tea-drinking at the bowling-green, where he first got acquainted with Mr Belton.'

'Mr Belton would never have troubled his head about such a little boy as George,' said Ellen, 'if it had not been for – you know what I mean, Mrs Dolly. All I wish to say is, that George's own good behaviour was the cause of our getting acquainted with this good friend.'

'And I am sure you were the cause, mother,' said George, 'of what you call my good behaviour.'

Mrs Dolly, somewhat vexed at this turn, changed the conversation, saying, 'Well, 'tis no matter how we made such a good acquaintance; let us make the most of him, and drink his health, as becomes us, after dinner. And now, I suppose, all will go on as usual: none of our acquaintance in Paddington need know any thing of what has happened.'

Ellen, who was very little solicitous about what Mrs Dolly's acquaintance in Paddington might think, observed that, so far from going on as usual, now they were living on borrowed money, it was fit they should retrench all their expenses, and give up the drawing-room and parlour of the house to lodgers. 'So, then, we are to live like shabby wretches for the rest of our days!' cried Mrs Dolly.

'Better live like what we are, poor but industrious people,' replied Ellen, 'and then we shall never be forced to do any thing shabby.'

'Ay, Ellen, you are, as you always are, in the right; and all I desire now, in this world, is to make up for the past, and to fall to work in some way or other; for idleness was what first led me to the gaming-table.'

Mrs Dolly opposed these good resolutions, and urged Maurice to send George to Mr Belton, to beg him to lend them some more money. 'Since he is in the humour to be generous, and since he has taken a fancy to us,' said she, 'why not take him at his word, and make punch whilst the water's hot?'

But all that Mrs Dolly said was lost upon Ellen, who declared that she would never be so mean as to encroach upon such a generous friend; and Maurice protested that nothing that man, woman, or devil, could say, should persuade him to live in idleness another year. He sent George the next morning to Mr Belton with a letter, requesting that he would procure employment for him, and stating what he thought himself fit for. Amongst other things, he mentioned that he could keep accounts. That he could write a good hand was evident, from his letter. Mr Belton, at this time, wanted a clerk in his manufactory; and, upon Maurice's repeating his promise never more to frequent the gaming-table, Mr Belton, after a trial, engaged him as his clerk, at a salary of 50*l.* per annum.

Every thing now went on well for some months. Maurice, on whom his wife's kindness had made a deep impression, became thoroughly intent upon his business, and anxious to make her some amends for his past follies. His heart was now at ease: he came home, after his day's work at the counting-house, with an open, cheerful countenance; and Ellen was perfectly happy. They sold all the furniture that was too fine for their present way of life to the new lodgers, who took the drawing-room and front parlour of their house; and lived on the profits of their shop, which, being well attended, was never in want of customers.

One night, at about ten o'clock, as little George was sitting, reading the history of Sandford and Merton, in which he was much interested, he was roused by a loud knocking at the house door. He ran to open it: but how much was he shocked at the sight he beheld! It was Mrs Dolly! her leg broken, and her skull fractured!

Ellen had her brought in, and laid upon a bed, and a surgeon was immediately sent for. When Maurice inquired how this terrible accident befel Mrs Dolly, the account he received was, that she was riding home from the bowling-green public-house, much intoxicated; that she insisted upon stopping to get a glass of peppermint and brandy for her stomach; that, seeing she had drunk too much already, every thing possible was done to prevent her from taking any more; but she would not be advised: she said she knew best what agreed with her constitution; so she alighted and took the brandy and peppermint; and when she was to get upon her horse again, not being in her right senses, she insisted upon climbing up by a gate that was on the road-side, instead of going, as she was advised, to a bank that was a little further on. The gate was not steady, the horse being pushed moved, she fell, broke her leg, and fractured her skull.

She was a most shocking spectacle when she was brought home. At first she was in great agony; but she afterwards fell into a sort of stupor, and lay speechless. 45

The surgeon arrived: he set her leg; and during this operation, she came to her senses, but it was only the sensibility of pain. She was then trepanned; but all was to no purpose – she died that night; and of all the friends, as she called them, who used to partake in her tea-drinkings and merry-makings, not one said more when they heard of her death than 'Ah, poor Mrs Dolly! she was always fond of a comfortable glass: 'twas a pity it was the death of her at last.'

Several tradesmen, to whom she died in debt, were very loud in their complaints; and the landlady at the bowling-green did not spare her memory. She went so far as to say, that *it was a shame such a drunken quean should have a Christian burial.* What little clothes Mrs Dolly left at her death were given up to her creditors. She had owed Maurice ten guineas ever since the first month of their coming to Paddington; and when she was on her death-bed, during one of the intervals that she was in her senses, she beckoned to Maurice, and told him, in a voice scarcely intelligible, he would find in her left-hand pocket what she hoped would pay him the ten guineas he had lent to her. However, upon searching this pocket, no money was to be found, except sixpence in halfpence; nor was there any thing of value about her. They turned the pocket inside out, and shook it; they opened evey paper that came out of it, but these were all old bills. Ellen at last examined a new shawl which had been thrust into this pocket, and which was all crumpled up: she observed that one of the corners was doubled down, and pinned; and upon taking out the yellow crooked pin, she discovered, under the corner of the shawl, a bit of paper, much soiled with snuff, and stained with liquor. 'How it smells of brandy!' said Ellen, as she opened it. 'What is it, Maurice?'

'It is not a bank note. It is a lottery ticket, I do believe!' cried Maurice. 'Ay, that it is! She put into the lottery without letting us know any thing of the matter. Well, as she said, perhaps this may pay me my ten guineas, and overpay me, who knows! We were lucky with our last ticket; and why should not we be as lucky with this, or luckier, hey, Ellen? We might have ten thousand pounds or twenty thousand pounds this time, instead of five, why not, hey, Ellen?' But Maurice observing that Ellen looked grave, and was not much charmed with the lottery ticket, suddenly changed his tone, and said, 'Now don't you, Ellen, go to think that my head will run on nothing but this here lottery ticket. It will make no difference on earth in me: I shall mind my business just as well as if there was no such thing, I promise you. If it come up a prize, well and good: and if it come up a blank, why well and good too. So do you keep the ticket, and I shall never think more about it, Ellen. Only, before you put it by, just let me look at the number. What makes you smile?'

'I smiled only because I think I know you better than you know yourself. But, perhaps, that should not make me smile,' said Ellen: and she gave a deep sigh.

'Now, wife, why will you sigh? I can't bear to hear you sigh,' said Maurice, angrily. 'I tell you I know myself, and have a right to know myself, I say, a great deal better than you do; and so none of your sighs, wife.'

Ellen rejoiced to see that his pride worked upon him in this manner; and mildly told him she was very glad, to find he thought so much about her sighs. 'Why,' said Maurice, 'you are not one of those wives that are always taunting and scolding their husbands: and that's the reason, I take it, why a look or a word from you goes so far with me.' He paused for a few moments, keeping his eyes fixed upon the lottery ticket; then, snatching it up, he continued: 'This lottery ticket may tempt me to game again: for, as William Deane said, putting into the lottery is gaming, and the worst of gaming. So, Ellen, I'll show you that though I was a fool once, I'll never be a fool again. All your goodness was not thrown away upon me. I'll go and sell this lottery ticket immediately at the office, for whatever it is worth: and you'll give me a kiss when I come home again, I know, Ellen.'

Maurice, pleased with his own resolution, went directly to the lottery office to sell his ticket. He was obliged to wait some time, for the place was crowded with persons who came to inquire after tickets which they had insured.

Many of these ignorant imprudent poor people had hazarded guinea after guinea, till they found themselves overwhelmed with debt; and their liberty, character, and existence, depending on the turning of the wheel. What anxious faces did Maurice behold! How many he heard, as they went out of the office, curse their folly for having put into the lottery!

He pressed forward to sell his ticket. How rejoiced he was when he had parted with this dangerous temptation, and when he had received seventeen guineas in hand, instead of anxious hopes! How different were his feelings at this instant from those of many that were near him! He stood to contemplate the scene. Here he saw a poor maid-servant, with scarcely clothes to cover her, who was stretching her thin neck across the counter, and asking the clerk, in a voice of agony, whether *her* ticket, number 45, was come up yet.

'Number 45?' answered the clerk, with the most

careless air imaginable. 'Yes' (turning over the leaves of his book): 'Number 45, you say – Yes: it was drawn yesterday – a blank.' The wretched woman clasped her hands, and burst into tears, exclaiming, 'Then I'm undone!'

Nobody seemed to have time to attend to her. A man servant, in livery, pushed her away, saying, 'You have your answer, and have no more business here, stopping the way. Pray, sir, is number 336, the ticket I've insured* so high, come up today?'

'Yes, sir – blank.' At the word blank, the disappointed footman poured forth a volley of oaths, declaring that he should be in jail before the night; to all which the lottery-office keeper only answered, 'I can't help it, sir; I can't help it. It is not my fault. Nobody is forced to put into the lottery, sir. Nobody's obliged to insure, sir. 'Twas your own choice, sir, Don't blame me.'

Meanwhile, a person behind the footman, repeating the words he had addressed to the poor woman, cried, 'You have your answer, sir; don't stop the way.'

Maurice was particularly struck with the agitated countenance of one man, who seemed as if the suspense

* This was written before the Act of Parliament against insuring in
lotteries.

of his mind had entirely bereaved him of all recollection. When he was pressed forward by the crowd, and found himself opposite to the clerk, he was asked twice, 'What's your business, sir?' before he could speak; and then could only utter the words – number 7? 'Still in the wheel,' was the answer. 'Our messenger is not yet returned from Guildhall, with news of what has been drawn this last hour. If you will call again at three, we can answer you.' The man seemed to feel this as a reprieve; but as he was retiring, there came one with a slip of paper in his hand. This was the messenger from Guildhall, who handed the paper to the clerk. He read aloud, 'Number 7. Were you not inquiring for 7, sir?'

'Yes,' said the pale trembling man.

'Number 7 is just come up, sir, – a blank.'

At the fatal word blank, the man fell flat upon his face in a swoon. Those near him lifted him out into the street, for air.

'Here, sir; you are going without your change, after waiting for it so long,' cried the clerk to Maurice; who, touched with compassion for the man who had just fallen, was following those who were carrying him out. When he got into the street, Maurice saw the poor creature sitting on a stone, supported by a hackney-coachman, who held some vinegar to his nose, at the same time asking him if he did not want a coach?

'A coach! Oh, no,' said the man, as he opened his eyes. 'I have not a farthing of money in the world.' The hackney-coachman swore that was a sad case, and ran across the street to offer his services where they could be paid for: 'A coach, if you want one, sir. Heavy rain coming on,' said he, looking at the silver which he saw through the half-closed fingers of Maurice's hand.

'Yes, I want a coach,' said Maurice: and bade the coachman draw up to the stone, where the poor man who had swooned was sitting. Maurice was really a good-natured fellow; and he had peculiar pity for the anguish this man seemed to feel, because he recollected what he had suffered himself, when he had been ruined at the gaming-table.

'You are not able to walk: here is a coach; I will go your way and set you down, sir,' said Maurice.

The unfortunate man accepted this offer. As they went along he sighed bitterly, and once said, with great vehemence, 'Curse these lotteries! Curse these lotteries!' Maurice now rejoiced, more than ever, at having conquered his propensity to gaming, and at having sold his ticket.

When they came opposite to a hosier's shop, in Oxford-street, the stranger thanked him, and desired to be set down. 'This is my home,' said he; 'or this was my home, I ought to say,' pointing to his shop as he let down the coach-glass. 'A sad warning example I am! But I am troubling you, sir, with what no way concerns you. I thank you, sir, for your civility,' added he, turning away from Maurice, to hide the tears which stood in his eyes: 'good day to you.'

He then prepared to get out of the coach; but whilst the coachman was letting down the step, a gentleman came out of the hosier's shop to the door, and cried, 'Mr Fulham, I am glad you are come at last. I have been waiting for you this half-hour, and was just going away.' Maurice pulled aside the flap of the hosier's coat, as he was getting out, that he might peep at the gentleman who spoke; the voice was so like William Deane's, that he was quite astonished. – 'It is – it is William Deane,' cried Maurice, jumping out of the coach and shaking hands with his friend.

William Deane, though now higher in the world than Robinson, was heartily glad to see him again, and to renew their old intimacy. 'Mr Fulham,' said he, turning to the hosier, 'excuse me to-day; I'll come and settle accounts with you tomorrow.'

On their way to Paddington, Maurice related to his friend all that had passed since they parted; how his good luck in the lottery tempted him to try his fortune at the gaming-table; how he was cheated by sharpers, and reduced to the brink of utter ruin; how kind Ellen was towards him in this distress; how he was relieved by Mr Belton, who was induced to assist him from regard to Ellen and little George; how Mrs Dolly drank herself into ill health, which would soon have killed her if she had not, in a drunken fit, shortened the business by fracturing her skull; and, lastly, how she left him a lottery ticket, which he had just sold, lest it should be the cause of fresh imprudence. 'You see,' added Maurice, 'I do not forget all you said to me about lotteries. – Better take good advice late than never. But now, tell me your history.'

'Now,' replied William Deane; 'that I shall keep till we are all at dinner; Ellen and you, I and my friend George, who, I hope, has not forgotten me.' He was soon convinced that George had not forgotten him, by the joy he showed at seeing him again.

At dinner, William Deane informed them that he was become a rich man, by having made an improvement in the machinery of the cotton-mills, which, after a great deal of perseverance, he had brought to succeed in practice. 'When I say that I am a rich man,' continued he, 'I mean richer than ever I expected to be. I have a share in the cotton-mill, and am worth about two thousand pounds.'

'Ay,' said Maurice, 'you have trusted to your own sense and industry, and not to gaming and lotteries.'

'I am heartily rejoiced you have nothing more to do with them,' said William Deane: 'but all this time you forget that I am your debtor. You lent me five guineas at a season when I had nothing. The books I bought with your money helped me to knowledge, without which I should never have got forward. Now I have a scheme for my little friend George, that will, I hope, turn out to your liking. You say he is an intelligent, honest, industrious lad; and that he understands book-keeping, and writes a good hand: I am sure he is much obliged to you for giving him a good education.'

'To his mother, there, he's obliged for it all,' said Maurice.

'Without it,' continued William Deane, 'I might wish him very well; but I could do little or nothing for him. But, as I was going to tell you, that unfortunate man whom you brought to his own door in the hackney-coach to-day, Maurice, is a hosier, who had as good a business as most in the city; but he has ruined himself entirely by gaming. He is considerably in our debt for cotton, and I am to settle accounts with him tomorrow, 55 when he is to give up all his concerns into my hands, in behalf of his brother, who has commissioned me to manage the business, and dissolve the partnership; as he cannot hazard himself, even out of friendship for a brother, with one that has taken to gaming. Now my friend, the elder Fulham, is a steady man, and is in want of a good lad for an apprentice. With your leave, I will speak to him, and get him to take George; and as to the fee, I will take care and settle that for you. I am glad I have found you all out at last. No thanks, pray. Recollect, I am only paying my old debts.'

As William Deane desired to have no thanks, we shall omit the recital of those which he received, both in words and looks. We have only to inform our readers, further, that George was bound apprentice to the hosier; that he behaved as well as might be expected from his excellent education; that Maurice continued, in Mr Belton's service, to conduct himself so as to secure the confidence and esteem of his master; and that he grew fonder and fonder of home, and of Ellen, who enjoyed the delightful reflection that she had effected the happiness of her husband and her son.

May equal happiness attend every such good wife and mother! And may every man, who, like Maurice, is
tempted to be a gamester, reflect that a good character,

and domestic happiness, which cannot be won in any lottery, are worth more than the five thousand, or even the ten thousand pounds prize, let any Mrs Dolly in Christendom say what she will to the contrary.

Sept. 1799.

A Note On Maria Edgeworth

Maria Edgeworth, 1767–1849, novelist, was born at Black Bourton in Oxfordshire, the daughter of Richard Edgeworth, MP for the Irish constituency of Edgeworthstown in County Longford. On her father's second marriage in 1773 she went to Ireland, but returned to England to attend school in Derby (1775–80) and London (1780–2). Her first published work, *Letters to Literary Ladies* (1705), was a defence of female education. The first volume of *The Parent's Assistant*, a collection of stories for children, appeared in 1776; its sixth volume was completed in 1800, the *Little Plays* being added later as a seventh volume. She collaborated with her father on the two-volume *Practical Education* in 1798, adapting and modifying the theories embodied in Rousseau's *Emile*. Her first novel for adult readers, *Castle Rackrent*, appeared anonymously in 1800 and was followed by *Belinda* (1801), *Modern Griselda* (1804) and *Leonora* (1806). The first series of *Tales of Fashionable Life* appeared in 1809 and the second, containing *The Absentee*, in 1812. Her later fiction included *Patronage* (1814), *Harrington* (1817), *Ormond* (1817) and *Helen* (1834). She completed the second volume of her father's *Memoirs* in 1820.

In 1823 she visited Scotland, being warmly received by Sir Walter Scott, an admirer of her work. He visited her at Edgeworthstown in 1825 and continued a regular correspondent. Although they did not otherwise come into contact, Jane Austen sent Maria Edgeworth a copy of *Emma* in 1816 and commended *Belinda* in *Northanger Abbey*.

Other titles in this series